Reading Paul Willis's poems in *Rosing fr*[...] hikes with an experienced, wise guide. I[...] and expecting each poem to show me a new vista. [...]g the way[...] always his soft, often humorous voice that keeps me attentive to what we're passing and assures me that we'll make it home safely.

—Thom Satterlee, author of *Burning Wyclif*

Whether dreaming of lost fingers or musing on the string of Willises in the *Dictionary of National Biography* or learning to see through the divided world of bifocals, Paul Willis captures the immediate and pushes it beyond the mundane to an unusual angle of vision. These poems reach beyond the occasional event to the most deeply redemptive insights.

—Jill Peláez Baumgaertner, Poetry Editor, *The Christian Century*

Readers familiar with Paul Willis's poems know to expect a delightful weave of keen observation, whimsy, and grace. He speaks as one willing to be amused, surprised, and taught by ordinary encounters with other living beings. And he loves a good pun, as good poets always do, because meaning always comes bearing secrets. The open secrets in these poems invite us all into a conspiracy of pleasure—in family life, in age and experience gratefully accepted, and in the wild, where we may still find renewal and revelation.

—Marilyn McEntyre, author of *In Quiet Light, Drawn to the Light,* and *The Color of Light,* a trilogy of poems on Dutch painters

Rosing from the Dead

Rosing from the Dead

··ᢀ[P O E M S]ᢀ··

PAUL J. WILLIS

WordFarm

SEATTLE, WASHINGTON

WordFarm
2816 East Spring Street
Seattle, WA 98122
www.wordfarm.net
info@wordfarm.net

Copyright © 2009 by Paul J. Willis

All rights reserved. No part of this publication may be reproduced, stored
in a retrieval system or transmitted in any form or by any means, electron-
ic, mechanical, photocopying, recording or otherwise, without the prior
permission of WordFarm.

Cover Image: iStockphoto
Cover Design: Andrew Craft

USA ISBN-13: 978-1-60226-004-7
USA ISBN-10: 1-60226-004-4
Printed in the United States of America
First Edition: 2009

Library of Congress Cataloging-in-Publication Data

Willis, Paul J., 1955-
Rosing from the dead : poems / Paul J. Willis. -- 1st ed.
    p. cm.
ISBN-13: 978-1-60226-004-7 (pbk.)
ISBN-10: 1-60226-004-4 (pbk.)
I. Title.
PS3573.I456555R67 2009
811'.54--dc22

                                                      2009019234

P 10 9 8 7 6 5 4 3 2 1
Y 14 13 12 11 10 09

Acknowledgments

I am grateful to Jack Leax and Jim Zoller, my first mentors in the art of poetry; to Al Haley, Bill Jolliff, Marilyn McEntyre, Heather Speirs, and Randy VanderMey, who have offered steady encouragement; to Marsha de la O, Perie Longo, Glenna Luschei, John Ridland, Bruce Schmidt, Barry Spacks, David Starkey, Phil Taggart, and Chryss Yost, my local editors month by month; to Catherine Hodges and Debra Rienstra, generous editors-at-large; and to Marci Johnson, my professional and painstaking editor at WordFarm. I am grateful to my wife, Sharon, for listening to Garrison Keillor read a poem every morning and telling me about it at night. And I am grateful to our children, Jonathan and Hanna, for opening doors to other worlds; to them I dedicate this book.

I also wish to thank the editors of the following publications, in which some of these poems first appeared:

Ancient Paths: "Emeritus" and "Pear Lake Ski Hut," *And What Rough Beast: Poems at the End of the Century* (Ashland Poetry Press): "A Miracle," *Appalachia:* "Telescope Peak," *Artlife:* "Where It Happened," *Askew:* "What I Can Hear," *Bark:* "Annie's Wish," *Blueline:* "Red, White, and Blue," *Books & Culture:* "Library" and "On Time," *California Quarterly:* "Signs and Wonders" and "What We Have," *Camas:* "Norman Clyde," *Christian Century:* "Bifocals," "Candles Waking" and "Visiting Hours," *Christianity and Literature:* "Rosing from the Dead," *Cider Press Review:* "Lizard's Mouth" and "What California and Alaska Have in Common," *Clackamas Literary Review:* "Filius" and "Nuclear Family," *Cresset:* "Early Morning," *DMQ Review:* "Trona Pinnacles," *Dog Blessings* (New World Library): "Higher Learning," *How to Get There* (Finishing Line Press): "The Fullback," "The Good Portion" and "Train Set," *Interdisciplinary Studies in Literature and Environment:* "Cottonwood Spring" and "Restricted Travel," *Kerf:* "Advent," "Birch Creek Tarn," "Santa Barbara" and "What He Can Do," *Kinesis:* "Four Fingers," "The Gospel Train" and "When You Say," *King Log:* "Still Here" and "The Way in Which," *Literature and Belief:* "Dictionary of National Biography," *Manzanita:* "At Cold Spring Tavern," *Mars Hill Review:* "Four," *New Song:* "Faith of Our Fathers," *OE Journal:* "Low Water," *Perspectives:* "Paul Jonathan Willis" and "Physical," *Poetry Depth Quarterly:* "Urban Planning," *Reflections:* "Across the Lawn," *Rock & Sling:* "Hidden Flesh" and "Trifocals," *Ruminate:* "Modern Languages," *Slant:* "Mind and Matter" and "What I Will Want," *Solo:* "Minimum Wage," *Stonework:* "Sierra Spring," *Weber:* "Old River" and "Orpheus Arrives from the Sea," *Where Icarus Falls* (Santa Barbara Review Publications): "Seven-Step Program," *Wilderness:* "Storm Clearing, Dusy Basin," *Windhover:* "The Finding." "Bifocals" has also appeared in *Glass Work: Art Glass, Windows, Marbles, Bottles, and Jars* (Pudding House). "Restricted Travel" has also appeared in *Dog Blessings* (New World Library). "Rosing from the Dead" has also appeared in *Books & Culture, Covenant Companion* and *Circuit Rider.* "What We Have" has also appeared in *Avocet.*

To Jonathan and Hanna

all before them

Contents

When You Say

When you say
my name has come up
several times, I hear it
gasp, emerging hopelessly
for air, then
sinking into voiceless ocean.

When you say my
name reminds you of certain tactile
peculiarities, husks of corn or a lost
thread of glass beads, I see it caught
between your palms like a stray moth,
murdered by your chance applause.

When you say my name
was shared by forebears on your
mother's side, I feel my life
already lived, spilled out perhaps
in Pickett's charge and only
gathered up in you.

When you say my name, just
say, just whisper it in my left ear,
I know that it is yours to give, that I
can take it back again but want
to leave it rising on the wind between us,
searching out a breath, a shape, a history.

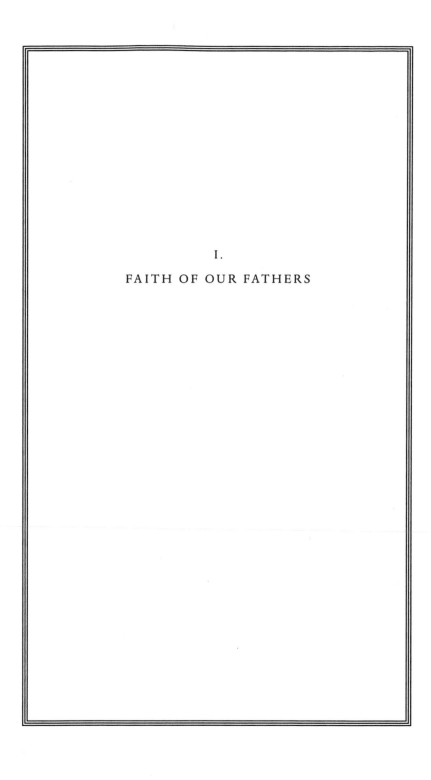

I.

FAITH OF OUR FATHERS

Paul Jonathan Willis

after Charles Harper Webb

As in the Apostle Paul, of course—
a big name, though the word means *little*.
I've always found it hard to pronounce,

hard to fit that *l* on the end, as if it were the paw
of a cat that couldn't scratch her signature.
But most preachers like Paul better than they like

Jesus, given the fact that Jesus told confusing stories
but Paul excelled in the prototype of the three-point sermon.
I am not too good at either, which would make me

more like Jonathan, that Horatio to David's Hamlet,
the selfless supporter, tending a little toward co-dependence.
Horatio was left to tell the story, at least what Fortinbras

would allow, but Jonathan went down with the ship,
fighting next to his father, Saul, against Matthew Arnold's
Philistines, which was Paul's name—Saul, that is—

before he changed it, something I would never do.
A friend of mine now calls me Pauly, who knows why,
but her husband recently hanged himself, and she

seems to need some terms of endearment in her life.
I've known people who change their names like leaves
in autumn, from Kathryn to Kate to Katie, just like that,

and a boy at the high school legally registered himself as
Trout Fishing in America, in honor of Richard Brautigan.
Where it all ends for me is Willis—son of Will, I have heard—

a British name, good for a guy who teaches
in an English Department, though at least half of me is German.
"Hey, Willis!" they say to me, and I like that, a last name

that could be my first, rising from what Paul the Apostle
regarded as the ends of the earth, that place
where his gospel was going.

Faith of Our Fathers

The faculty ate lunch and sang today,
a dark day in the old chapel. We lent
our less than thousand tongues

unto a fortress mighty as it's ever been,
and though there were brave women too
we bellowed like bass organ pipes,

joining mostly our forefathers
in echoes of their hallowing,
our brief and particular stanza.

So many rich voices among us,
grave and deep and reverberant,
and this was a great comfort to me—

to be still a child after all, still surrounded
by grown men growling low
in their unmistakable harmony.

Mind and Matter

My father kept a human brain, pickled and beige
in a musky jar, on a shelf in his university office.
"Is it thinking?" I asked.

It floated, serene
in the softness of its tangled lobes,
tabula rasa perhaps, but convolved.

Was this my father's *memento mori*,
the skull and candle over his desk
to recall the *vanitas* of this world?

Or was it the glory of his skill
in the biological sciences, the mark
of his ability to name and enter each small cell?

Poor *pia mater*, we did not know
whose you were, and so you foundered
for both of us,

wrecked and raised,
then set adrift, a ship in a bottle,
poised to sail this starless sea.

The Gospel Train

In those days a pale pastor
came to our house. It could
have been Saturday afternoons.
The pastor was young, and very sickly.

He stood in the basement
watching my father extend his model railroad
well into the infinite future,
a wired and coded eternity.

Together they planned a millennium
of closed loops, just after
the tribulation of box cars
jumping the tracks and splintering

on the linoleum floor.
Whether such a fall as this
could justify God's ways to men
presented a tangible problem of evil.

And the layout itself—was it created
by design, or did it merely evolve
with the years? A little of both,
my father assured him.

The pastor would leave satisfied,
uncoupling from a cordial handshake
at the door. He died young.
I hoped that was not part of the plan.

Where It Happened

Recess, and we were playing four square,
the ball spanking in and out of cold puddles
redolent of asphalt, of November rain,
our hands wet and black and numb.

It was Ragan Humphrey, the tallest boy
in the third grade, with the reddest hair
and the biggest freckles, who brought
the news. "Hey," he told us, cutting in line,

"President Kennedy just got shot.
Shot dead." *"No cuts,"* we said.
"Come on," we said. The ball bounced
out of bounds, but no one ran to get it.

The Cubs

After little league one evening, riding his bike
with his oiled glove swinging sweet from the handlebars,
coasting the trail past broken-down barns,
through the paling whisper of wild oats,
he saw the bear and her young by the river,
rising out of the shallows like a visiting team
come back for a rumble. He pulled up short,
leaned into a cottonwood like a rookie hugging first base,
and watched the mother crouch
before a backstop of willows while the smaller ones
crossed the field to ravage a mound of blackberry vines.

His path lay beyond them. He calculated
his chances then of stealing second.
The cubs on the mound. Mama bear behind the plate.
The sun setting in stands of oak, and the crickets
harassing invisible batters. As in most games,
for a long time nothing happened.

Then a warm breeze picked up at his back,
and the massive catcher swiveled her snout
in his direction, raised her paw. The cubs balked.
He was out of there, pedaling behind that blackberry
patch like a runner beating a sacrifice, like a
wild pitch, like a line drive fouled into the bullpen.
And he never looked back to catch the score
until it was dark, until he was quite safe at home.

A Miracle

I am twelve years old, sitting in the dollar seats
in the end zone, closest to the beige coliseum.
It is November, perhaps. It is 1967. It is raining

lightly, a gray sky, the usual for autumn in Oregon.
It has been raining all week long. The field
before me stretches away without lines, without

hash marks. It is a perfect churn, a cauldron,
whipped into a seething of mud. The players rise
and fall before me as dark and streaming

apparitions, bubbling to the surface, sinking, all
wearing a filthy slaver. All except one. Whenever
this one takes the ball, whenever he tries to cut

the corner and sprint upfield, the men in the crowd
around me cry out, "O.J.! O.J.!" The men sound
very worried, as if someone were breaking

into their homes. They are only relieved when O.J.
slips in the mud or is just knocked down from behind.
But a miracle. He gets up—every time, when he

gets up—his uniform is shining, spotless, gold and
crimson: no dripping grime, no ooze of smudge, no
smear of earth and water, not even a trail of blood.

The Fullback

I was always amazed to see him there
in the balcony of our Baptist church,
not singing much but hunched forward
attentively for the whole sermon
while rain ran downfield on the aging roof.
His massive arms must have been aching
after another patented day of three yards
in a cloud of mud. For me, that blocky,
crewcut head, that earnest face,
dumb with respect, brought Saturday
into Sunday, the secular to the sacred.
I cheered him on each lumbering carry,
and I cheered him now, back in our huddle.

Nuclear Family

There was a man at the Baptist church,
he taught physics at the university
and built a ranch on a hill of oat grass
out of town, and he sang tenor solos in a warbling
voice of fine control, fine as the contour of his
brow and black, curled hair. He sang that solo
every summer, all the way to Los Alamos
to split the atom again and again, and every
summer his blonde wife, she had an affair,
and his two boys, they slashed some tires.

On Time

Mr. Roscoe, we called him. (So fun to say: *Roscoe.*)
He worked for the Southern Pacific. When he came
to our Sunday School, he sat down carefully
on the stage, then rescued a gold
railroad watch from his back pocket and said
with a wink that he was always *on* time.
That might have been his exact job, to keep
the trains on time, except he told us how much
more important it was to keep time with eternity.

Mr. Roscoe was a little man, dark hair
slicked back, beginning to bald. The kind
that came every Sunday from the neighboring
mill town with his round-faced wife
and his round-faced daughters—who,
in terms of fashion, were not exactly up-to-date.
This was the 1960s, but the Roscoe girls
wore floral-print dresses and wavy hair,
same as the pictures of country people
in my parents' wedding book.

But one day, Mr. Roscoe was not on time
for church. He was not even there, and did not
ever come again. His wife and daughters
kept arriving now and then, but sat
beneath their rosy skirts in a way that said
they did not wish to speak with us.
We were finally told that the late Mr. Roscoe
had not died, he had just run away
with a Southern Pacific secretary. Boarded a train,
presumably, sitting gingerly on that hard seat.

Train Set

The train hums to itself in the dark
like the plastic engine my father
holds to cut our hair. It worries

itself in a closing circle, a dog
chasing its own tail.
These are the pieces of bent

track my brother has allowed
to me, the brother who wails
when our father tries to ride

his hair with the locomotive,
the brother who would
do anything for a dog.

My father comes and lets in light,
he finds straightaways for an oval.
Now there is room for a tunnel,

for the gondola to disappear,
taking away its tubs of milk
and bringing them back into the open.

Filius

after Naomi Shihab Nye

From my father I have gained the ability to sharpen
pencils, to straighten my desk, to load the back
of a station wagon with boxes that fit just so.
We print neatly, and take off points for grammatical errors.

Did I tell you he was a teacher? And that I am too?
His field was biology. Charles Darwin's grandfather
put all of natural history into one long poem.
This was in the eighteenth century. He could
have been both of us, but he wasn't.

From my mother I have taken a certain heaviness
in my flesh. Big bones. That is the German
part of me. Also, a certain shame about my body.
It was not a Christian thing to dance. In spite of my
occasional efforts, my body still believes this.

A few months before I was born, my mother
came down with polio. For most of a year, she lay
on a bed. It was not often she could hold me.
To this day, I am not too good at hugging people.
But I can hold them in this poem. My mother,
my father, I can hold you in this poem.

Early Morning

Just outside, the helicopter lands again
on the hospital roof. You sleep
through the wash of the rotor,

pulling up breath through thickened lungs,
past the narrow feeding tube, impediments.
Let me not disturb you, Mother, just as you

would let me curl in cribs on darkened afternoons.
Love bears it out by many a bedside
in this place, and why not ours?

Why not this slow and steady breathing,
this watching over you by dawn,
this waking to familiar clouds?

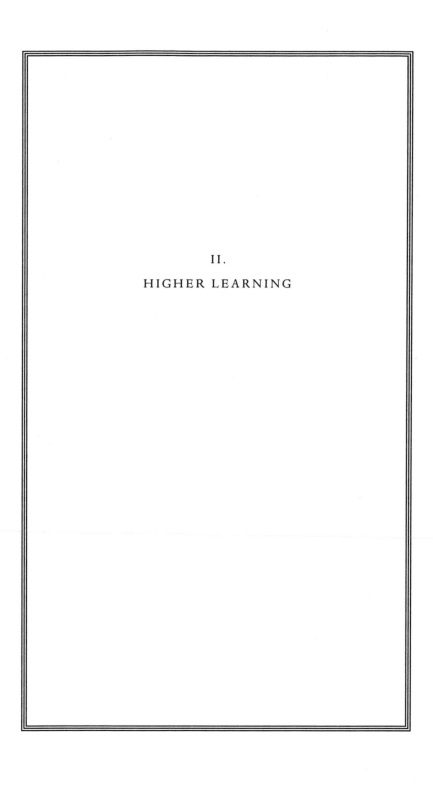

II.

HIGHER LEARNING

The Way in Which

The way in which the human body
is capable of cupping itself about what is
gone, the womb squeezing its own hollow,

the tongue pushing into the gap
of the broken tooth—how flesh
gathers into need, and word brims emptiness.

The way too in which every gesture
is insufficient, all words of loss
lost, each hand a broken sieve.

The way in which we finally have
to be content with open sky
where once, bright windows.

Hidden Flesh

These rising moons beneath translucent
fingernails—all day they circle this globe
of thought and rest from their orbits at night.

Five leftward, five rightward, open secrets
that never touch, preserved
in pink museums of shell.

Think of them as the most intimate
parts of your body, the universe—
erogenous zones

no lover has ever found,
where no foot will ever make
a small step for humankind.

Four,

says Jung, is the perfect number. That's why
the church venerates Mary, because the Trinity
wasn't enough—the feminine fourth leaf on the clover
wafting behind the four dread horsemen.

That's why there are four gospels, and four states
on the West Coast, and four years between presidents,
except for the ones who happen to die in person
or in reputation. That is why the years leap

every fourth February, why a mile takes four laps,
and four minutes to run if you're fast. That's why
there are four seasons, and four limbs on the human body,
and why the thumb is different from the other fingers,

the odd one out. That's why there are four people in my
house, four walls around us, and four corners to this page.
When I go, that's why there will only be four hairs left
on my head. God, I think, will still be counting, quaternally.

Possible Endings

The paper said she was struck
twice in the back of the thigh
by an arm-thick rattlesnake.

It left no poison—no use killing
what it couldn't eat. Soon after,
already snakestricken, the same woman

was diagnosed with breast cancer.
She was 42. Almost anything can
occur at 42, though that was a year

I personally happened to survive.
Our retriever died of a lump inside
his jaw last month—he was nearly 11.

We laid him on the grass and felt
his welcome breathing disappear
inside our hands. A man I once

climbed mountains with is scheduled
to leave this world and his wife
and daughter after his next birthday.

Lymphoma. He called to say
he was so sorry about our dog.
I think he enjoyed the chance to express

some sympathy. I wrote him a letter
after that, possibly my last to him.
I didn't know how to close.

The bottom of the page
approaching, I just put,
"Good night, sweet prince."

And then, crabbed into the margin,
"That's Horatio to Hamlet.
And they were friends."

Four Fingers

I dreamed you lost the fingers
of your left hand. It was snakebite
or burn or infection, some strange cause,
but there they weren't, those fingers
that belonged to you the week before,
that belong in the natural course of things
to virtually every eight-year-old boy.
Being righthanded, you got along
without them okay, writing and drawing and
opening doors, and you had that thumb
to oppose against your lonely palm,
but once in a while you cast a silent
glance at that hand, and felt your difference.

In my dream your Uncle Dave sat
facing you, the one who lost his fingers
and thumbs to a cold mountain years ago,
the one who signs his Christmas gifts
"from Santa Paws." You were like him now,
you had forty percent something
in common, but neither one of you
mentioned it. I wondered if now you belonged
to him more than you belonged to me,
if loss unites and loss divides,
if the gift of your birth is year by year
taken away.

What He Can Do

after Elizabeth Holmes

Bounce a flat basketball between his legs
without looking. Dive through a breaking wave.
Find anything on the Internet in six seconds.

Batter a drum till the walls shake.
Sag his jeans to the lowest
inch possible. Refuse to sing.

Polish his cymbals until they shine
with his own reflection. Call out the note
of the vacuum cleaner—a middle C.

Skate off a curb with both hands
deep in his pockets. Sleep till noon.
Hold a dog the way a dog wants to be held.

Annie's Wish

Murphy, Annie's black toy poodle, is learning tricks.
So far he can sit, shake, roll over, lie down, and stand
on his hind legs for longer than I'd think possible.

Right now he is learning about his feelings.
When Annie says, "Be sad," he is supposed to put
both paws over his eyes. So far, Murphy is not very sad.

We are talking now about weddings,
Annie's brother just having come home from one.
"Annie," I say, "when you get married, if Murphy

were to be in the wedding, what would he do?"
"What do you mean?" Annie says. She looks worried.
Annie's father clarifies. "What part would Murphy play,"

he says, "in your wedding—if he was in it?"
Then Annie knows: "Murphy would be the flowers."
"Ah," I say, "the flower dog—

he would carry the flowers down the aisle."
"No," says Annie. "Murphy would *be* the flowers."
She picks him up and presses him close.

"I'd carry Murphy instead of holding a bouquet."
What a beautiful day for a black dog.
When Annie gets married, be sad, Murphy, be sad.

What I Will Want

Some years from now, my bones aching,
I will want to wake up again on this ordinary
morning of fog, my daughter applying blush

before her first period of chemistry, my son
sleeping in after a late night on his drum set,
waiting until the last to get to the high school

in the eight minutes he says that it takes.
My wife finally shakes him to inquire about
ride-sharing plans for the day, a dentist appointment,

the need for a lunch, and he replies in low
tones, nearly past his need for a mother,
though she not past her need for him.

The dog barks, just one year old, eager to pass
through closed doors and bite down
on a newspaper, a sock, a pillow,

to gain the touch of rising children,
just as I will want that touch, this
hour of waking, before I sleep.

The Good Portion

*Mary has chosen the good portion, which shall not be
taken away from her. Luke 10:42*

Is it waking to this calm morning
after a night of dry winds?

Is it scrambled eggs, the ones with cheese,
or the hot glaze of a cinnamon roll?

Is it the way you laugh over breakfast,
that generous gift, your laughter?

Is it rinsing the plates and pans in the sink?
Or leaving them in a cockeyed stack,

these things of use, these things of beauty
that will not be taken away?

The Planet of Your Desires

When I stand in the sea and feel the waves
pull back and forth across my thighs,
that is the way you come to me

when only one star is left
to say farewell to the night.
That star is the planet of your desires,

which renew themselves like the hot
winds of evening that shake
the blinds in every window.

We leave the doors open, then,
to save ourselves from the rattling
of locks, and reef the blinds

to navigate the pulse of the moon.
Where she takes us, that
is the place that we were going.

Candles Waking

When I get up in the night to stifle
a cough with hot tea, and make my way
through the black terrain of the dining room,

there are candles waking in the dark,
open eyes that never sleep:
the blue glow of digital minutes

winking under the television,
the coffee maker, the microwave.
A laptop beams its single pulse,

and the mouse beside it arches
over the red flame of a beating heart.
The rat scratching away in the attic

suddenly seems superfluous,
the stars outside the sliding door
a vestigial redundancy.

When I wake in the night and cross
to the greening numerals upon the stove,
I voyage within my own fixed sphere,

my lonely festival of lights.

Cutting Edge

My writing students sit with me
in a smart classroom. It is called
smart because a data projector
hangs from the ceiling by a post,
a screen the breadth of a white barn

supplants the grass of the chalkboard,
small black speakers perch
like crows, and a podium stuffed
with VCR, DVD, and CD players
looms like a scarecrow in the front.

On the pierced side of this podium
lie silver wounds for hooking up
the milking tubes to whole herds
of Macintosh. Our classroom is so smart
we hardly know how to escape it.

Sometimes we hide up in the hayloft
and stroke the inky shadows of mice.
Sometimes we suck on a poem,
get out the rusty sickles of Time,
whatever it takes to put off buying the farm.

Modern Languages

On your left, small tapestries of France and Spain.
We're a small college, that's what gets taught here.
Occasionally the native tongue of Goethe too,

but not so much. I am told my great-grandfather
mortgaged his farm to build a German Baptist church
in Anaheim. They stopped holding services in *Deutsch*

during the First War, and stopped for good in '42—
not so popular just then to be a Fleischmann or Urbigkeit.
I only know a phrase or two. *Der Wienerschnitzel.*

Sergeant Schultz on *Hogan's Heroes*—"*Jawohl,
Herr Kommandant!*" I wouldn't be able to sit down
with my *Urgroßvater,* ask him why he risked the farm.

I do possess a rage for order—line up little sticky notes
in straight rows across my desk; eat all of my green beans
before starting in on the meat loaf, then the potatoes.

Could this be the German tongue asserting itself,
nonverbally? My wife is half-German as well—Pennsylvania
Dutch, in fact. But when she braids her fine blonde hair,

she could be the edelweiss of alpine meadows,
the barmaid of beer gardens way off in Bavaria,
a place where we have never been. Perhaps that is why

the whole of our marriage remains a remote mystery,
why I will never say to her, *mein Liebchen,
mein Wellensittich, meine eigene liebende Leitzel.*

The Finding

Green tennis balls lie blooming on the lawn.
I find them in the morning when I park
beside the courts, beneath the dripping oaks.
My office is nearby. Before I go
to see what waits upon my desk that day,

I wet my shoes in grass and pluck the flowers
of fore- and backhand plants that knew no bounds,
that grew in the exuberance of youth
beyond the pale, past where the eye could see.
I hold them soft between the thumb and palm,

and feel them damp, and tight, and full of spring,
then toss them in the footwell in the back,
where they will circle like a dog at rest
and sleep the day away while I go on,
while I go wilt awhile and serve in-bounds.

Emeritus

My old professor took me by surprise:
he quoted St. Augustine with his eyes.
"You see? You see?" he said to punctuate
his periods lest they scatter inchoate.
I came, I saw—or thought I did years back.

But now I only feel the lonely lack
of feeling in his conquest—I that heard
my own experience was quite absurd,
that burned with his idea of a college,
am burdened now with older kinds of knowledge.

Higher Learning

I put him out four times this morning,
let him fetch the paper, walked him
round the block, but still the puppy
peed twice on the kitchen floor—
great, spreading puddles of gold
that soaked into the doormat.

He looks at me with the eyes
of an assistant professor up for tenure,
hopeful about his classroom evaluations,
his latest research. If nothing else,
he thinks we should retain him for his warm
collegiality and service to the institution.

But he is merely plotting where to poop next.
No limit to the academic freedoms
of a dog these days, no end
to the publication of alimentary happiness.

Library

From the blank hush of my cubicle, I listen
to the library. Someone is coughing,
someone confiding plans to a phone.
In the cloistered cell next to mine,
the sweet sound of a page turning.

As a child, on summer afternoons,
I sometimes rode with my father
down the hill to his laboratory.
He would dissect his newts and frogs,
and I would walk under bigleaf maples
and dark sequoias to a library of seven floors,
to the coolness of the basement and its many books,
a permanent prospect of borrowed joy.

Those were the days when people
did not think to talk in libraries,
and the air kept a silence I could taste
inside my spine. I would rejoin my father
at the appointed hour profoundly pleased
with where I had been, carrying with me
sacred space, a way of dwelling.

After college, living at home a month or two,
I took a job in the public library
next to the Sixth Street railroad tracks,
where the clatter of trains and the quiet
of words negotiated a broken truce.

Shelving each book, I paused to consider
chance details about the author, a rundown
on the plot. Then I might see how
the first chapter began, and how the second.
I am there in the aisle when the locomotive
thrums down the street, its whistle calling
to get on with the real work,
the book still resting in my hands,
the hopeless pleasure of chapter three.

Bifocals

Now I live in divided and distinguished
worlds, joined by an equatorial smudge,

the common murk of middle earth.
Now I learn to bring my book under

my nose, to bow my head in reverence
to observe my footing on the stairs.

Now the drawing down of blinds,
the narrowing of near and far,

the clarifying closure of these unhinged
doors of perception, cleansed but cloistered.

Dictionary of National Biography

In the *DNB* lie twelve grave persons by my name,
most of them John, Robert, or Thomas,
not counting Richard Willis (from Ohio, it turns out),
who wrote the carol "It Came upon a Midnight Clear."

Resting in peace are three physicians, an alchemist,
a lone dissenting minister, a bishop (finally of Winchester),
a schoolmaster who liked to translate English proverbs
into Latin, an early archaeologist, a justice of the king's bench,

a struggling painter, an antiquary, and a Renaissance
inventor of shorthand. One of the doctors specialized
in mental derangement, and treated George III in his madness.
He insisted on gentle measures, and made himself popular

at court. Women called him "the image of simplicity."
Another discovered a scheme of arteries in the brain,
ever after celebrated as the (rather intimate) Circle of Willis.
The justice was sent far afield to Canada and New

South Wales, where he quarreled with almost everyone,
same as at home. The painter favored the picturesque,
and was best remembered for rendering cattle onto canvas;
Victoria paid him handsomely for one of these. My favorite,

however, is the eighteenth-century antiquary, who gave away
his vast estate to whim and charity, bit by bit, and died at last
a ragged beggar. According to Sir Leslie Stephen,
"He was a great oddity, and knew nothing of mankind."

Trifocals

I would like to say the world is now
richly Trinitarian. But to tell the truth,
it has simply become more bureaucratic,

a place where even my right hand
must be submitted in triplicate.
If there be something spiritual

about my vision, I must confess
to constant doubt as to
who it is I am seeing now:

the distant Father,
the proximate Son,
the most intimate Holy Ghost.

I glance above my rims to see
the hills, their ceanothus bloom,
only to have them disappear.

My help comes from closing my eyes
and thinking then of silver coins,
cool against the lids, the lashes.

Physical

"You would not believe," my doctor said,
"what they let my daughter do at Notre Dame.
She has a job there in the library—
she's just a freshman. Anyway, she mends
old books that suffer from collapsing spines.
Any problems breathing? Any catch
when you inhale? I think your lungs are clear—
no sign of that pneumonia from last fall.
We'll take an X-ray to be absolute.
But what they let her do is bind a book
that Christopher Columbus once had owned.
His signature was on the title page.
Just drop your trousers if you would, that's fine.
Bend over. Yes, you'll feel a slight discomfort.
Columbus, think of that, his very hand!
Clear sailing there, just leave your trousers off.
Put them beside your shirt and lie down here,
flat on your back. Look up. Breathe normally—
I'll check your abdomen for tenderness.
Cough if you can. That's right. But do you know
what one of my professors said to me
the last time I was back for homecoming?
He said the gospels were not written by
the four evangelists, that there's no chance
that Matthew, Mark and Luke and John composed
a single word of their supposed books.
That bothered me, that nearly stopped my heart.
I mean, if that's not true, well then, what is?"
His face loomed over mine; about his eyes
a tic of agony did wretched things
to his cool countenance. "What do you think?"
"Well, there's debate," I cautiously replied.

"No manuscripts?" he pressed. "No autographs?"
"I think a parchment fragment of St. John
was once uncovered in a pile of sand,
say, from the first or second century—
but just a few bare words, a phrase or so."
That's all I thought to say. His busy hands
hung limp beside him, faithless to their task.
He gave a nod, then turned back to my chart.
"That's it, then," he said brightly. "You look good.
Make an appointment for a year or two.
You're healthy as they come." But we both knew
the body of my text lay all too frail,
a signature we could not mend or bind.

Visiting Hours

A friend of theirs had been festering
like an old sandwich, rotting
a little before disposal. They had to come,
but it got to where they held their breath
before they stepped inside the room.
The wife remembered how anything
with mayonnaise had to be refrigerated.

Even a sack lunch in an office was suspect
if stored under the desk for a morning:
egg salad was the worst.
The husband recalled a tiny door
in the stone wall of an English church,
stage right from the modest altar—a place
for lepers to take communion. Only part

of a soul could pass, and precious
little of the smell. The wife and husband
talked with their old friend like this, backing
off from his suppurations, unwilling to think,
This is our body, unwilling to think,
Dust to dust, slipping their elements of decay
into the outer cold and darkness.

Rosing from the Dead

We are on our way home
from Good Friday service.
It is dark. It is silent.
"Sunday," says Hanna,
"Jesus will be rosing
from the dead."

It must have been like that.
A white blossom, or maybe
a red one, pulsing
from the floor of the tomb, reaching
round the Easter stone
and levering it aside
with pliant thorns.

The soldiers overcome
with the fragrance,
and Mary at sunrise
mistaking the dawn-dewed
Rose of Sharon
for the untameable Gardener.

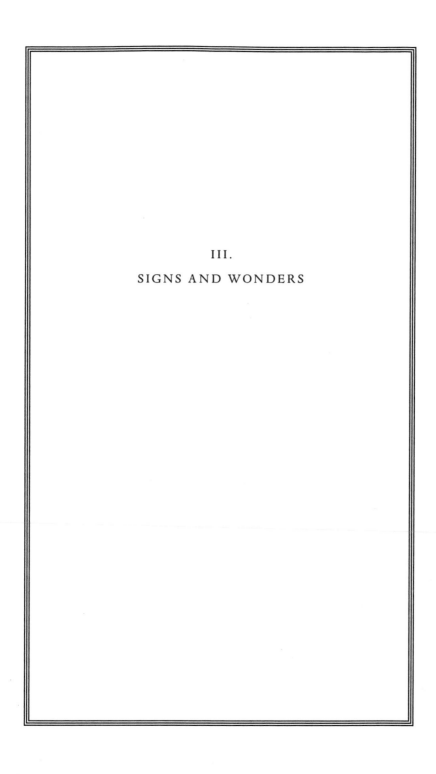

III.

SIGNS AND WONDERS

Minimum Wage

Along the far edge of the lawn, juniper shrubs
entangle the mower, wrapping the blades with pliant boughs.
A cough, a silence, a burst of Sabbath pungency.

Oak leaves in autumn, wet with rains,
can do the same, and have to be raked
through the tall grass like the combing out
of the hair of mermaids before the cutting,
and then the dank locks have to be raked again,
gathered in piles—your palms, your arms, your soles
stained with the blood of grass and mermaids.

Summer, whole acres of weeds have to be grubbed,
down on your knees in mud and clay
as if in prayer for their demise, the burn of thistle
within your fist, the slime of slug, the sweet
shine of poison oak. It can rain all June,
just as it does in the fall, but on dry August
afternoons, as you slice and sickle the crooked
heat between wild oats, between blackberry vines
in dusty thickets, a breeze will come
across the mountains from the Pacific
and quicken the maze of sweat on your brow.

You will drop your scythe, place your blistered hands
on your hips, and look up at the sound of wind
in the heaving branches of Douglas fir,
a sound that spreads across the valley like rescue,
like the quick return of your own breath.

Across the Lawn

the clean white trunk sways upward
in come-hither fashion, lithe to the eye
and limbing gently to the air.

When we climbed the bigleaf
maple in the empty lot next door,
or the Douglas fir by the driveway,
it was but practice in embracing

the human form. Getting to that
first branch was always the problem,
but once there, courtesy of a running start
or a heave of interlocking hands,

we soon found grip and sap in plenty.
There was something in us
that wanted to go all the way,
to take the slender arms of sky—

but something too that kept us modest
in our affections, cradle and all.
And who is to say it was not love—
love in its first and purest form?

And now this whitening tree that beckons—
foot to crevice, palm to pitch,
knees still shaking above the ground.

Hilltoppers

I was fifteen, maybe—new at climbing the Cascades,
at slogging up endless slopes of snow,
or in this case, an endless ridge of scree and talus,
a full seven thousand feet from Pamelia Lake
to the summit of Mt. Jefferson.
Was it my brother that was with me?
Or a couple of friends from high school?

Whoever it was, by late morning, the air growing thin,
the stones began to swirl like leaves,
like dry leaves in an autumn wind.
For an acre or two the crest of the ridge
was whispering with soft orange wings:
                   butterflies.
We were tired by then, our lungs burning.

We had no idea why butterflies had come
this far from timberline. But they brushed our boots,
caused our hands to float in new and strange directions.
Years later, I found the species in a book:
Oeneis nevadensis, Sierra Nevada arctics,
                  hilltoppers
that contrive to meet and mate on peaks and ridgetops.

So convenient, this, a pre-arranged spot with a view.
No guesswork. No showing up early
for study hall. No waiting around after the dance.
Just a long, simple, determined climb,
like the one we were on, we brothers,
we boys, breathing hard to make the summit,
to tell the girls all about it.

Crossing the Canyon

Over and over, our grandmother played
the *Grand Canyon Suite* on the phonograph
in her upstairs parlor in Pasadena.

"These are the mules," she would say.
"And this the storm. And now,
you see, the storm has gone."

In that railway tunnel in Disneyland
the Grand Canyon also appeared in pastel
spaciousness, a bighorn on every ledge.

On Sunday evenings, in black and white,
Walt retold the river journey of Major Powell,
a minister of the interior
like his English namesake, John Wesley.

And that picture of him in the museum on the rim—
one-armed, bearded, astride his horse—
a good deal like you, my brother, no hands,
pausing to wait for me on the trail.

Pear Lake Ski Hut

I had a vision one March day.
  It happened where we lay
Asleep in the Sierra in a hut.
   The door was shut,
But sunshine through the windows made a way.

It was new morning after storm;
  The sky was not yet warm.
Six feet of snow lay sparkling under eaves,
  Where nothing grieves;
A freshness and a farness found each form.

Outside the hut our ski tracks ran
  A brief and curving span
Around a knoll and disappeared from sight—
  A snowy height—
Then wandered back to where our trail began.

And though the door was closed, we stood
  Upon the threshold good
And welcomed the bright morning on the knoll.
  The gray birds stole
Among the needles of our little wood.

Behind us rose a matterhorn,
  A slope to gently warn
The possibility of avalanche,
  But tree nor branch
Gave clue nor sign of danger to be borne.

Far otherwise. For round the knoll
On quick skis came the soul
And body of a friend from out the grave.
God may us save
As she was saved that morning free and whole.

I saw her plucky smile, her eyes,
As if the grisly guise
Of death had melted like a glaze of ice.
What could suffice
More than her grace in coming in this wise?

But then behind her came another;
It was my older brother
In full possession of his hands and feet.
With joy we greet
Him too to make our few, both one and other.

Then came a friend who was estranged;
Now glad and wholly changed,
He skied up laughing to our fellowship,
Not in the grip
Of lust and lies in which he darkly ranged.

Then came another pair and more
Of old friends to our door,
All young and fresh, and free of tears and hurt—
Not our desert,
But what we had been granted, what in store.

And though this hut slept only ten,
There was still room again
For each who came; and there was room for all
In that great hall,
Those lovely living women and those men.

This was my vision. You can say
It was not so, or lay
Your wager on the odds it will not be.
But as for me
And for my stony hut, we wait that day.

Sierra Spring

No storms since February, then two burning
weeks of March, winter snowpack going fast.
The hutkeeper at Pear Lake said eleven feet this year:
the lodgepole by the door marks four feet,
maybe six, depending how you rim the well.
The surface dense with cones, twigs, branches,
needles—my skis a wax museum of flora.

Streams flowing, bursting through. We took
a chance on a rotting bridge over Silliman Creek,
got lucky. Granite slabs shedding their scarves.
In the afternoon, the slope settles, unsettles,
the hollow *whomp* of layers collapsing underfoot
like the heartsick shock of love dismissed,
Ophelia returning her tokens.

—Sequoia National Park

Birch Creek Tarn

Clumps of whitebark wave in the wind
among boulders that greet no one at all.
Snowbanks back away

from gopher cores and shooting stars—
not the flowers, not yet, but the fleshy
fingertips of leaves, finding the air

like lowland crocus in early spring.
Tawny grass lies dazed and dead,
hardly knows its second chance,

the sound of water slipping from
field to field of snow, awakening
roots, awakening the hidden seeds.

—John Muir Wilderness

Telescope Peak

Fresh wind tumbles in from Olancha
on the west horizon, gift from the ocean
even here. By afternoon, skies wash milky

with the spume of alkali, salts pillaring
out of the flats below the level of the sea.
On this high ground, among remnant

cornices of snow, bristlecones root themselves
like an ancient people, chesting the blow,
tasting with needles what goes by.

—Death Valley National Park

Orpheus Arrives from the Sea

It is seldom calm on this high ridge.
The Jeffrey pine are flattened and splayed
by wind from the west, from the ancient
play of air above the distant ocean.

The needles make aeolian choirs,
each loft of singers rooted in place
above the muted, sunburnt hum of manzanita

while boulders listen expectantly
from the forest floor, unwilling
to settle for nothing, ready to roll.

—San Rafael Wilderness

Trona Pinnacles

Just here, in this long train of towers,
a ring of brown bent monoliths

surrounds a campfire in the desert.
They hulk like druids in the wind,

their slow rising from underwater
calcium springs no stranger

than the torturous journey
of stones on logs

across the plain of Salisbury.
What is there here to honor

and to know? The tufa rock is sharp
to the hand, a shock to the eye.

Across the salt and sand
of this long empty lake, these towers

frame that void for which they stand,
and which they stand against.

—Mojave Desert

Santa Barbara

Those pink condominiums on the far hill
in the sunset, they could be the hotels
waiting for you on Boardwalk or Park Place.

Palm trees line the beach like twenty-dollar bills
tucked just under the edge of the board.
And out to sea, silhouetted against the fog,

the gray hulk of a battleship, or perhaps
a destroyer, movable piece in a global game.
Everything was already in play

when you got here. Who's ahead?
How much will it matter when the sun
finds the ocean, and screams?

Urban Planning

Panamint City had one street, a mile long,
a thousand feet higher at one end
than at the other. Two hundred stone houses.
Fifteen hundred law-evading citizens.
This was 1875. Seven-hundred-fifty-pound balls
of silver rolled down the main street
and out of town in sturdy wagons—
too heavy to steal on horseback.
In 1876, flash floods killed two hundred
inhabitants and washed away their civic remains.
Panamint City went downhill from there.

Storm Clearing, Dusy Basin

Erratic boulders strew this slab
of granite sloping into meadow—
dice cast on a polished floor.

The game is never up.
Dark clouds roll through the peaks
to flush new gold,

enough to stake our claim,
to hold a rainfly for another day,
a night, another chance to spend

this mottled sky, this whorled pine,
this violet spray of penstemon
that never knew its delicate gamble.

—Kings Canyon National Park

Questions at the Time

Does willow grow by the lake, or does granite?
    Does water tremble there, or the sky?
        Does the wind blow, or is it the breath
            of a bear speaking quietly? Does a cloud

leave this shadow in place, or is it the backside
    of God? Which sun could be shining
        except itself? What eye of heaven
            tasted by the rich, red lip of this horizon?

—Kings Canyon National Park

Seven-Step Program

1

Purple sage, meadow, morning.
Red-winged blackbird rides a perch
on yellow mustard, rides another,
swaying, calling: *I have found it,*
I have found it.

2

A trail, a ledge, a buzzing rattler,
fat and folded in his coils. No room
for both of us. I climb below, regain
the path beyond. Kind of him
to sound a warning, say goodbye.

3

Oak limb crashes in the forest,
merges with the sound of sun
in afternoon. I hear for all
the absent people, walking,
sleeping, in other canyons.

4

Alder roots and tendrils reaching
down to water. Trout are waiting in
the rapid. Long and patient
fishing, this—the wetting and the
slow release of many lines.

5

Wind all night, moon
and then bright stars,
a planet, glowing
like the Coulter pine cones
lost in embers at our feet.

6

Small snow taps
the tent at dark, spats
of ice from Jeffrey pine.
Mist, fog coming where
the bear drop over the rise.

7

After fire, manzanita
waving arms like wailing
women. Wet green
under the roots, wallflower
re-imagining the flames.

—San Rafael Wilderness

Still Here

These green-stemmed lilies
still come crowding out of the garden
into the winter day's last sun.

They so want the life they have,
the pulp and pith within the fleshy
solstice of their reach and bloom,

still stalking after light and air, still
leafing there. Quite unlike the purple
flower of one man's face,

the pallid anthers of his eyes, when
they found him hanging after church, uprooted,
all uprooted from our common longing.

What I Can Hear

Deep in the night, the freight sounds
its horn by the crossing just below the zoo.

That is where the homeless camp, where
one might kneel on the tracks

to make an end. That part I cannot hear
from three miles up the hill, just as

I cannot hear the leopard sigh, the waves
sift onto the beach. But the clatter

of the wheels on the rails, I can hear that.
It doesn't stop, it doesn't stop, it doesn't stop.

Low Water

The creek finds pool and pool without
the intervening falls, without the rapids,
appearing and appearing in its dark
and stricken silences.

Capillary sounds beneath the stones
decide the question of continuance;
dry crush of bay leaves and of sycamore
perplex the canyon, salt and powder
stillnesses.

Sandstone boulders wait in muted
flesh, as they so often do. They were rolled
here once and will be rolled again—
they know and yet believe they will be
rolled away from glassy mouths,
from autumn tombs.

Lizard's Mouth

It is only a short walk. From the best angle, what
you see is a tilt of sandstone yearning west
with a hollow of hunger under the prow—

for all the world a rock in the eternal act
of gaping after the wanton gods.
The chase of lovers on Keats's

urn is not so terrible as this.

The yellow palate is mazed
with a pocky web, a membrane,
the tongue long melted into air—

into pure air that stretches into light
to taste the winter bloom of manzanita,
the circling sea, the salt-glazed islands.

Red, White and Blue

In early March, the toyon berries hang
in embers, fading under pale explosions
of ceanothus—a froth, a kindling,
winter offering itself to spring.

We walk beneath their intertangling,
unsure of this season in our lives.

Then overhead, a scrub jay passes
suddenly from bough to bough,
for that one moment hidden
in its own allegiance to the sky.

Signs and Wonders

A day and a half and nine miles up the trail,
in a hollow below Hurricane Deck,
where a seep descends its algae stairs
and a slick of sandstone rises
on the other side—just here,
an iron platter leans against the roots of an oak
with arrows scratched to points beyond:
San Diego, London, Paris, Baghdad even—
with the comical miles etched beside.

Ambling through this wilderness
on a Presidents Day weekend,
we were just beginning to forget
these places of supposed importance,
the urban killing fields of Iraq, the ones
we have read about every morning,
though blessedly not that morning, waking
to news of alder groves and quiet streams.
But now this rusty rearrangement,
a reminder that you could get there
from here, that no one can walk away.

—San Rafael Wilderness

What California and Alaska Have in Common

The gophers were here first. So were
the Chumash. If an Indian boy came tunneling
up beneath the peppers and tomatoes,
we would gas him too.

Some of the men might wrap themselves in bear hides
and prance about on all fours.
That kind we could shoot.

On a cruise ship in Glacier Bay, a Tlingit woman
takes the stage in the Vegas lounge
to speak about the cedar canoes,
the smokehouses for the salmon.

We bury her with our applause,
then spill on deck to watch the ice
explode the water, just for us.

Cottonwood Spring

Just below the cathedral shade of Cottonwood Spring,
slow water sliding down the face of an altar
into a thick, grassy nave—just below, by the sandy wash,
by the tangle of salt bush and mesquite, a bench of granite
holds a pair of mortar holes, ground smooth into the rock.
Each one swallows my flesh from forearm to fingertip.

The sign says, *Think about how long it took
to wear the holes that deep.* So I think about it—
the women leaning low to their work with quivering dugs,
stone pestles firm in their grip, the smashing
and smashing of beans and seeds into flour.

And yet, elbow-deep in their history, I can't quite
make the reach. For one thing, these were women.
The Cahuilla men were probably off somewhere else, as I am.
I don't even understand what women of my own time
do together when they labor side by side—
rinsing lettuce under a faucet, or conferring
over the draft of an essay, or rolling their eyes
in synchrony at a meeting in the dean's office.

I do know that women often speak together in their tasks.
But maybe the Cahuilla were silent. Perhaps they
had tasted all they needed to say by breakfast,
or perhaps they did not talk till supper—or perhaps
they did not take these meals, not even lunch,
but nibbled the beans and seeds as they worked.

But if the gossip flowed like the spring over its stone step,
if it eddied among the grasses of each family member,
the roots of the tribe—who was barren, who with child,
who caught coupling under the mistletoe of the ironwood tree—
if the laughter blossomed out like the golden tongues of brittlebush,
like chia, aster, desert poppy, if it hung in the air like the creamy
plumes of Mojave yucca, like the scarlet tips of the ocotillo,
if it sank into the sand of the wash, never to come up again,
I know they did not speak of me.

—Joshua Tree National Park

Frank Felt Gets Married

"Don't let that picture fool you," Blakley said.
He leaned back in his study, slipping down
thick glasses on his weathered face to show
eyes hard to know the truth about the past.
"Frank Felt, he lived way up the Sespe near—
you know Pine Mountain Inn?—you do—well there,
just near that spot, away back up the Sespe.
And every year he'd make the ride to Hemet
to play the part of a Franciscan Friar
in Helen Jackson's pageant—every year,
a pageant all about the early days.
Helen Hunt Jackson—yes—she lived there then.
You see the robe is gray, and that's because
the friars' robes *were* gray in mission days—
not brown as now. And every year Frank saw
a nice young lady, down by Hemet there.
She wanted him to ask a certain question.
He never did. Frank never thought she'd want
to live way up the end of some horse trail.
One moonlit night back there up at his cabin,
Frank hears the hooves of horses out his door.
He steps outside, and coming up the trail—
it was leap year, I should've told you that—
he sees four horses in the moon, all gray.
The first one carried the witness. On the second,
the minister, and on the third, the bride.
The fourth, it was her packhorse, loaded up.
'You haven't asked me, Frank,' the lady says,
'but since it's leap year, I thought I'd ask you.'
That's how Frank Felt got married." Blakley's eyes
were misty now, not hard with scrutiny.
Before I left he said, "It's not the same—

it's not the same now as it was back then.
The friars' robes were gray in mission days."

At Cold Spring Tavern

The man on the fiddle recorded himself
with a foot pedal, then topped his echo
in higher notes that moved like squirrels

across a tapering limb of oak. We stood
in the dark and watched him through
an open window, and he looked up

and nodded the way my college roommate
used to do. I dreamed last night
of a long-dead uncle, the one who packed me

all the way to Graveyard Lakes in the Sierra.
He stood there calmly, muscles rippling
through his legs like notes of preternatural music.

"You've been out walking some," I said.
He just looked at me and smiled,
the other side of an open window.

Restricted Travel

I descend the canyon just a little,
jumping boulders in the stream, but my dog,
my aging golden retriever, is none too good
at scrambling down. A drop of four, five feet
sets him barking fresh refusals. Now that he's almost

nine years old, he's given up alternate routes.
So he stands there, barking,
and I'm just a bit ahead, just getting to the better part,
where the channel steepens in pools and falls
and the canyon opens out of oaks and laurel

into sunshine. From here you can almost glimpse
the sea, the islands round the far horizon.
But I climb back into the shade and tell myself
that next time I will come alone, knowing I won't.
As I cradle him up by his quivering haunches,

or ease him out of a pool by his collar, I think
that this is why I came. And he stands on a tangle
of alder roots and shakes himself, and we
are very wet together, and this is how we share
the creek, this is how we bless the canyon.

What We Have

There are still fall colors here, even in Santa Barbara:
the bright crimson of toyon berries, clustered
against the paling sky, the chartreuse mottling
of sycamore leaves and yellowing rust of bay,

of laurel. Along each path, bleached memories
of poison oak, a hardening of its arteries
while tender grass appears behind
November rains. And in the high folds of the ridge,

well above the waterfalls and already hidden
from the sea, the inland bloom of cottonwoods,
holding up their blazing hands
and giving all they owe to the wind.

Advent

The ticks begin to ripen here
in late November, dangling plump
and juicy from the chest and jowls
of our retriever. Once, on
a three-day hike, I found them hanging

off his lips, rooted firmly
even there. That was in
December in a brushy canyon,
California wilderness.
Late at night, in my sleeping bag,

I feel them take me on the hip
or place their heads beneath my thigh.
What is it that I owe them there?
What measurement of blood and self
is given or is theirs by law?

I do not wait for oil or flame
but pluck them by the hindmost parts,
and so their bodies are broken in me,
the dark remembrance of their seed
left festering for weeks to come.

In morning, when we steal from camp,
they drop down softly in our hair
from trees that overarch the path.
They patter gently for our flesh.
Their quality of mercy is not feigned.

Norman Clyde

Back in the sixties a friend of mine
surprised him in the High Sierra,
stumbling into his hidden campsite.

Clyde must have been 80 by then,
well finished with his first ascents.
Stacks of kindling lay about,

and Greek and Latin classics flapped
on slabs of granite. Norman turned,
one eye a red socket, his hands

laving a small, glass sphere. What he held
flashed quick in the sun like mountain summits,
earth's fire, Prometheus still unbound.

Old River

You March and muddy Tualatin,
fern-lover, moss-mover, tender
of your many alders,

I watch you glide to the Willamette,
to the Columbia, to the Pacific.

Your slippery bank is where
I stand. From here I greet you.
There you say goodbye, goodbye.

About the Author

Paul J. Willis is a professor of English at Westmont College in Santa Barbara, California. He is the author of three chapbooks of poetry, one of which, *The Deep and Secret Color of Ice,* was selected by Jane Hirshfield as winner of the 2002 Small Poetry Press contest. His first full volume of poems, *Visiting Home,* was published by Pecan Grove Press in 2008.

His poems and essays have appeared in *Poetry, Wilderness, The Best American Poetry 1996* (Scribner's), *The Best Spiritual Writing 1999* (HarperSanFrancisco), *The Best American Spiritual Writing 2004* (Houghton Mifflin), and *The Best Christian Writing 2006* (Jossey-Bass). His essays are collected in *Bright Shoots of Everlastingness: Essays on Faith and the American Wild* (WordFarm, 2005). With David Starkey, he is co-editor of *In a Fine Frenzy: Poets Respond to Shakespeare* (University of Iowa Press, 2005). Forthcoming from WordFarm is his four-part eco-fantasy novel, *The Alpine Tales.*